D1362161

THIS WAY, THAT WAY

Antonio Ladrillo

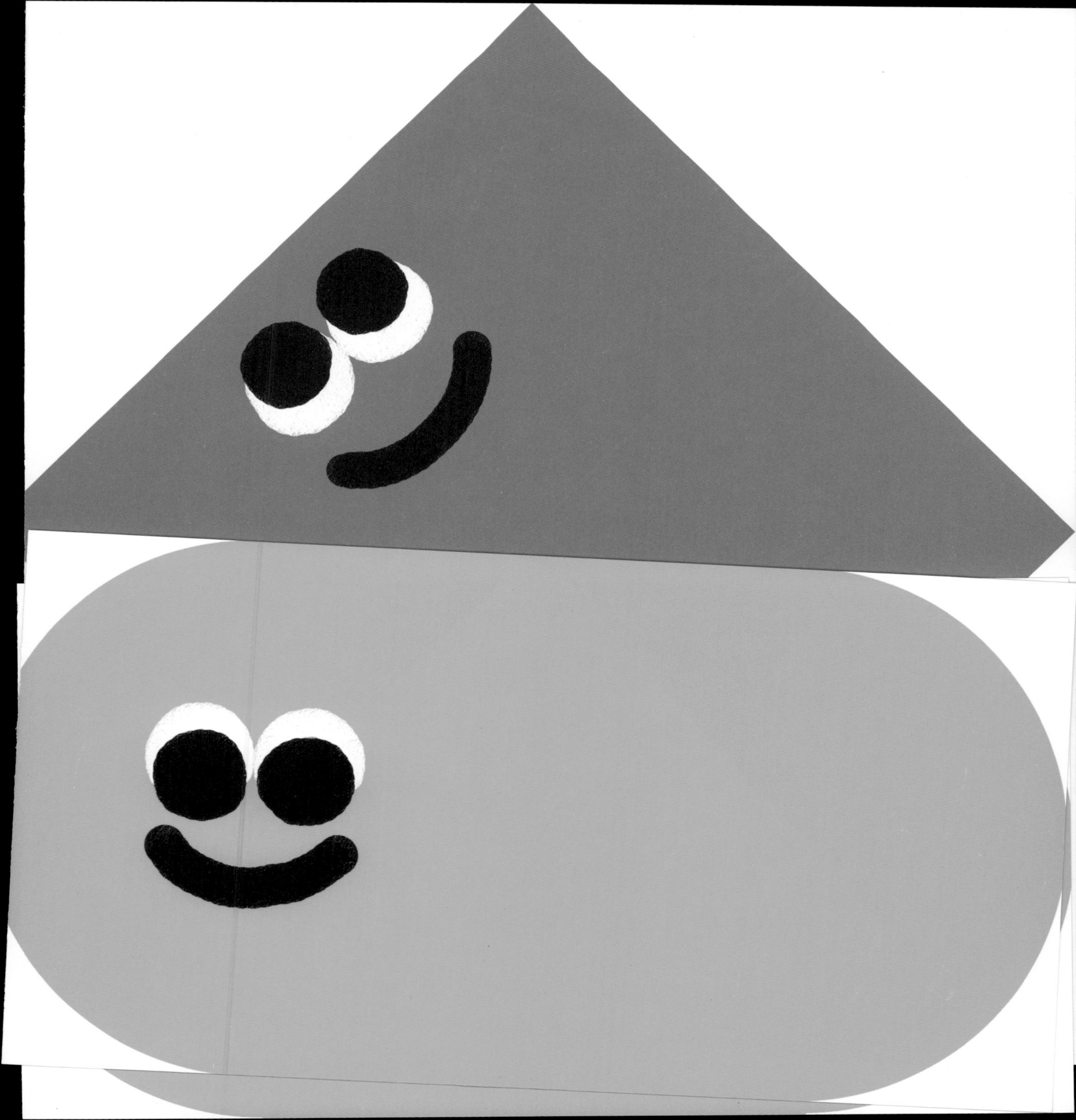

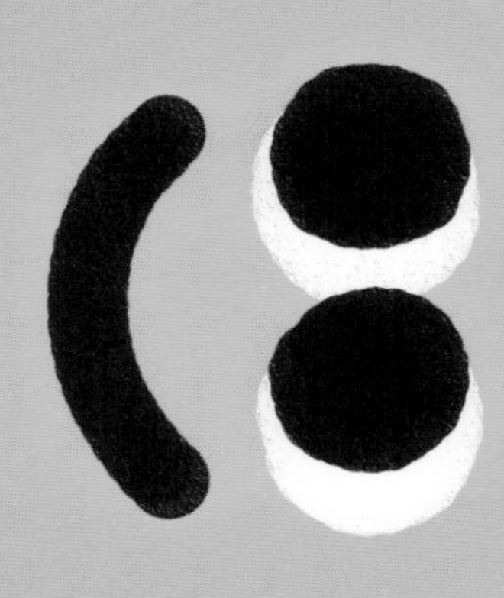

First published 2017 by order of the Tate Trustees
by Tate Publishing, a division of Tate Enterprises Ltd,
Millbank, London SW1P 4RG
www.tate.org.uk/publishing

A catalogue record for this book is available from the British Library

ISBN 978 1 84976 451 3

Distributed in the United States and Canada by ABRAMS, New York
Library of Congress Control Number applied for

Printed and bound in China by Toppan Excel Printing Ltd